USBORNE GUIDE TO SOCCER

Simon Inglis

Edited by Susan Meredith

Contents

With special thanks to Peter Dunk

Illustrated by
Rob McCaig, Paul Buckle, Graham Round and Kevin Lyle

Designed by Graham Round and Kim Blundell
Design revision by Robert Walster

Basic soccer skills

This book explains some of the skills, tricks and tactics used by top-class soccer players. It will help you to get more enjoyment out of watching skilled players in action. You will have more fun playing too, and your game will improve as you start using all the tips and hints. Throughout the book, there are some good ideas for practice and a special section on games you can play without a full team. It is hard to play well unless you are fit, so some fitness routines, based on those used by the professionals, are also included for you to try.

On the first six pages of the book,

you can see how the players in a side build up attacks and score goals, once they have got possession of the ball. The next sections talk about the equally important skills needed to win the ball in the first place and to defend the team's goal from attack.

The sections on tactics and teamwork in this book should help you to get into the habit of looking critically at a match as a whole, rather than concentrating only on the area of the pitch where the player with the ball is.

The picture sequences on pages 27-29 will make it easier for you to

spot the tricks that skilled players often perform at high speed, during a game.

You can also use this book as a reference for the laws of soccer, to find out how the major, international competitions are organized and to discover how leagues are run.

On these two pages, you can see the basic skills a player has to have when he is in possession of the ball. During a game, it is unusual for any player to have the ball for more than two or three minutes, so it is essential that he puts those minutes to good use.

Passing

The aim of all players is to help their team score goals. This means they must be able to pass the ball accurately to each other without losing possession to the other side. There are several different sorts of pass and players have to vary the type they use to suit the situation. Here are some examples.

Notice, when you are watching a match, how the passer keeps his eyes on the ball at the moment of impact and uses his arms to help him balance, as shown in these pictures. Notice, too, how he has to get the right power behind the pass so that his team-mate has the best chance of controlling the ball easily.

1 Ball struck in middle with inside of foot.

Arms out for balance.

Kicking foot turned out from hip, almost at right angles.

Supporting foot beside ball, pointing towards target.

A pass with the inside of the foot is a good way of getting the ball over a fairly short distance accurately and quickly, while keeping it low.

2 Ball struck towards bottom to give lift.

Kicking foot swept well back.

Instep

Supporting foot just behind and to side of ball to give lift.

A pass using the instep, with good preparation and a long follow-through, gives the ball power and distance. Here, you can tell from the position of the player's supporting foot that he is preparing to loft the pass.

3 Toes jab at bottom of ball.

Player leans back slightly and has supporting foot to side of and just behind ball to give lift.

You will see players lifting the ball over the head of an opponent close in front by making a "chip" pass. The toes jab at the underside of the ball, with no follow-through. This makes the ball rise steeply.

4

Ball flicked with outside of foot between little toe and ankle bone.

A pass with the outside of the foot is not usually as powerful as one with the instep. But it can be disguised until impact is made and so deceive the opposition. Here, as the challenger closes in, the ball is simply flicked away to the side.

Wall pass

One player passes to a team-mate and runs round his opponent into a space where he can receive a return pass from the team-mate. He has used his team-mate rather like a wall to bounce the ball off. This pass is also known as a "one-two".

2

Control

When a player receives a pass, he has to stop or "trap" the ball and bring it under control at his feet very quickly, often in a space which is crowded with other players battling for possession.

Notice how many different parts of the body skilled players use to trap the ball. Whichever part is used, the basic technique is always the same. At the moment of impact, the part of the body hit by the ball is relaxed and pulled back to cushion and absorb the force of the ball. If it is kept rigid, the ball simply bounces off the body.

As in passing, the eyes are kept on the ball and the arms are used for balance.

Ball blocked with inside of foot

Foot pulls back to absorb impact and smother bounce.

Body in line with flight of ball, chest puffed out, arms braced.

Shoulders brought forward, chest relaxed and pulled in to let ball fall.

Screening the ball

Player's body shields or "screens" ball.

If a player has possession of the ball, but cannot pass immediately, he often has to protect it from an opponent by "screening" it. This means putting his body between the opponent and the ball. The player in this picture has shifted the ball to his outside, away from the opponent, and is now ready to pass with the outside of his foot.

Head down

Ball kept close to foot.

Running with the ball

Running with the ball is not as simple as top international players make it look. The player has to gain space fast, keeping the ball under close control at his feet without breaking the rhythm of his stride. At the same time, the player has to keep glancing up to see if there is a team-mate he can pass to or an opponent who is about to challenge him.

Practices for passing and control

You can practise passing with one or two friends. Vary the sort of pass you use but always try to be accurate. Get into the habit of trapping and passing quickly. Always keep moving and pass over longer distances as you improve.

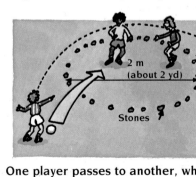

2 m (about 2 yd)

Stones

One player passes to another, who is inside a circle. He has to trap the ball while an opponent challenges, and then he has to pass back to the first player, who runs round the edge of the circle. Take it in turns in the different positions and keep moving.

Into attack

As soon as a team gains control of the ball, it looks for an opportunity to move forward into attack, trying to gain ground and create chances for scoring. The "forwards", or "strikers" as they are often called, have the main responsibility for attacking. But every player is allowed to score goals, so all the players in a team must be prepared to join in an attack. In the same way, every member of the opposing team will try to stop the attack.

On these two pages, you can see some of the ways in which teams try to break through the opposition's defence.

Dribbling

1 Dribbling the ball past a defender requires very close ball control and involves a variety of tricks and disguises to fool the opponent. In this picture, the dribbler pretends to attack on his opponent's left side. This is a "feint".

2 Hoping to stay with the attacker, the defender starts to move to his left. As soon as the dribbler sees his opponent is fooled by the feint, he shifts his body weight on to his right foot and transfers the ball to his left foot.

3 With his opponent caught off-balance by the sudden change of direction, the dribbler gives the ball a rapid tap with the outside of his left foot and swerves past on the opponent's right. The opponent cannot recover in time to challenge.

4 The dribbler accelerates away. Notice how his body has stayed perfectly balanced over the ball, with the ball close to his feet, throughout the manoeuvre. At the same time, a dribbler always has to be aware of other players' positions.

Improve your dribbling

About 2 m (or yards)

Set up a row of obstacles, such as garden canes and plastic bottles. Move the ball in and out with a series of light taps. Use the inside and outside of your foot. Practise with both feet. Time yourself and see if you can beat your own speed.

Giving an attack width

An attack with width has a greater chance of beating the defence. This stretches the opposition across the pitch and gives the attackers the choice of using the centre of the pitch or either of the sides.

Notice how the attackers run into spaces.

Giving an attack depth

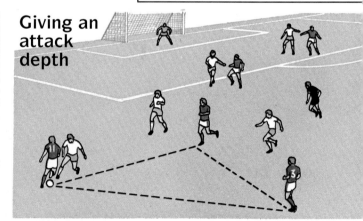

Depth also increases the moves attackers can make. Here, you can see how the red attackers are forming a triangle. Number 3 is a defender who has come forward to join the attack. He is ready to take a pass, pick up a loose ball or run back into defence.

Beating the defence

1 Wing play

An excellent way of beating the defence is to take the ball along one of the edges of the pitch (the 'wings'). Then the player should kick it or "cross" it from the wing into the goal-mouth, for a striker to run on to. Picture 1 shows the attacker crossing

2

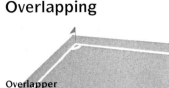

early to a striker up in front. Defenders are caught off-guard, too far away from their own goal to prevent a shot. Picture 2 shows the attacker crossing the ball from the goal-line, and playing it back into the path of a striker who is running in, ready to shoot.

Overlapping

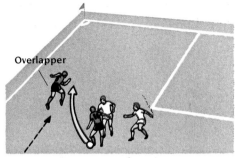

If an attacker out on the wing cannot cross the ball because an opponent prevents him, the attack can be kept moving by a pass to an overlapping player who runs up on his outside. The overlapper may than be able to find space to cross.

Cross-over

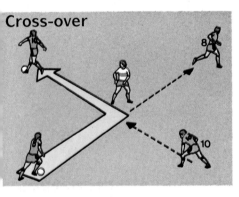

This is a move to confuse the defence. Number 8 is in possession, but at the cross-over point he runs over the ball, leaving it for number 10, who takes it in a different direction. Number 8 continues his run to increase the confusion.

1 Corners

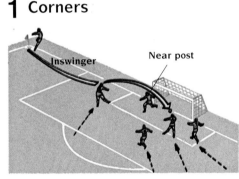

Corner kicks* provide opportunities to beat the defence. Here, the ball goes to the near post, where an attacker heads it on to other attackers coming in at the far post. This corner is called an "inswinger" because it bends towards the goal.

2

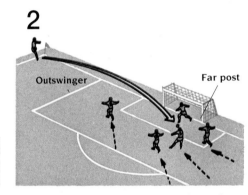

Here, the ball is kicked directly to the far post. One attacker often makes a decoy run across the goal, drawing defenders after him and giving players at the far post more room. This corner is an "outswinger" because it bends away from the goal.

1 Free kicks

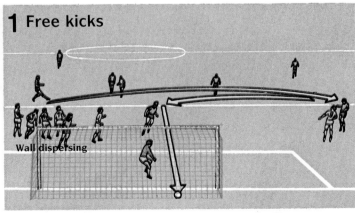

As at corners, there are many ways of attacking at a free kick*. Here, defenders expected a shot at goal, but the kick is sent wide and, before the players forming a wall have had time to disperse, it is headed back across the goal to a loosely marked striker.

2

Players acting as decoys at free kicks, making dummy runs and confusing the defence, help to increase the chances of scoring.

Here, number 11 attempts to draw defenders after him and so leave the ground clear for a pass to be made to number 6.

*See page 22 to find out when corner kicks and free kicks are awarded.

Scoring

Shooting from the ground

Attacking play does not necessarily lead to goals being scored, unless a team has players who can shoot and head accurately. A low, hard shot with the instep is one of the most common ways of scoring. Accuracy is more important than power, though some players can make the ball go at over 112 km/h (70 mph).

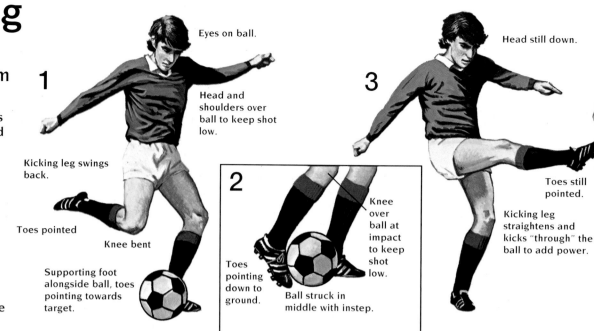

1 Eyes on ball.

Head and shoulders over ball to keep shot low.

Kicking leg swings back.

Toes pointed

Knee bent

Supporting foot alongside ball, toes pointing towards target.

2 Knee over ball at impact to keep shot low.

Toes pointing down to ground.

Ball struck in middle with instep.

3 Head still down.

Toes still pointed.

Kicking leg straightens and kicks "through" the ball to add power.

1 Heading a goal

Attacking heading* requires accuracy. If the ball comes at the player from an awkward angle, he has to use his neck muscles to flick it in the right direction (as in this picture). He must take care always to meet the ball with his forehead, both for accuracy and to lessen the chances of injury.

Improve your shooting

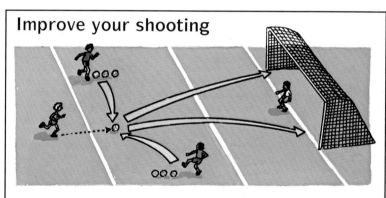

Two players take it in turns to feed balls at different angles and heights for a third to run on to and shoot. The shooter should practise with both feet and always shoot while the ball is still moving. If there is no one to act as goalkeeper, shoot at a target on a wall. Take it in turns in the different positions.

2

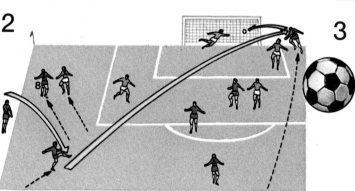

Here is a typical attacking move leading to what is known as a "far post header". The opposition players concentrate on the throw-in on the near side of the pitch and are diverted by number 8's decoy run. Meanwhile, a striker runs upfield on their "blind side" and scores from an early cross.

3

You will see spectacular goals scored by diving headers. An attacker who dives for a low cross is difficult to challenge because his body stretches across the path of the ball.

*For more about heading, see page 8.

Head kept down.

Leg straight at follow-through.

Body leans slightly backwards.

Shooting from the air

Shooting at goal "first time", that is, without controlling the ball beforehand, is an essential skill for strikers, who are almost always under pressure from opponents.

Notice how top-class players use different parts of their foot to kick the ball when it is still in mid-air (a "volley") and just as it lands (a "half-volley"). On the right is a volley with the instep.

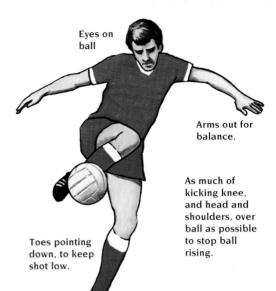

Eyes on ball

Arms out for balance.

As much of kicking knee, and head and shoulders, over ball as possible to stop ball rising.

Toes pointing down, to keep shot low.

Lifting the shot

Shots into the top corners of the goal are the most difficult for goalkeepers to save, but it takes a lot of practice to place them accurately. The player above leans back slightly to lift the ball towards a top corner, but keeps his head down to stop it rising too high and missing the goal.

Swerving the ball

Ball spins this way

A ball which swerves and spins is hard for a goalkeeper to stop. To shoot like this, kick the side of the ball with the outside of the top of your boot, with your foot turned in. For swerving the ball with the inside of the foot, see page 18.

Scoring moves

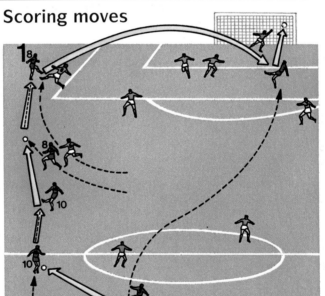

Good strikers do not simply wait for chances to score. They play a part in all attacking moves, even if they do not touch the ball. Here, number 9 starts the move, passes to number 10 and runs upfield to score from a well-timed cross from number 8. Get into the habit of watching the pattern of the players on the field, instead of concentrating on the ball, and see how a team builds up its attack.

In this picture, number 6 passes to number 10. Number 10 then passes to 8, who has run up from behind, ready to have a shot at goal. Notice number 9's decoy run across the penalty area to confuse the defence and momentarily block the goalkeeper's view. Watch out for players running without the ball and see how they are playing an important part in the game.

Winning the ball

When the opposition has the ball, a team's main job is to regain possession, or at least defend its goal and prevent the other side from scoring.

The "backs" and, if there is one, the "sweeper" (see page 10) have the chief responsibility for defending but, just as every player might join in attacks, every player has to be prepared to defend, using the skills shown on the next four pages.

It is especially important for a team to be well organized in defence. The slightest mistake can lead to a goal being given away.

Tackling

Tackler

Tackler

Body braced on impact.

Supporting leg bent.

1 Front block tackle

Facing his opponent, the defender pushes the inside of his foot against the middle of the ball, "blocking" it against the opponent. Bending his knees for balance and strength, he braces his foot and puts his full weight behind the tackle.

2 Side block tackle

The tackler blocks the ball against his opponent's foot as in the front block tackle but, because he approaches from an angle, he cannot get his body behind the ball and so his tackling leg takes all the impact.

Heading

In defensive heading, distance is often more important than accuracy, because players have to get the ball well away from their own goal. Notice how they try to get the ball to a team-mate at the same time, whenever possible.

Here is an example of a powerful header.

Arms used to gain height and momentum.

Back arched

One-footed take-off to get height.

Legs kicked up behind.

Ball punched hard with centre of forehead. Eyes open at impact.

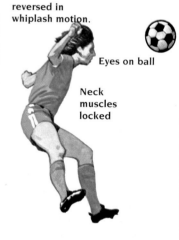

Arch of back reversed in whiplash motion.

Eyes on ball

Neck muscles locked

Challenging

Tackling is only allowed when the opponent has the ball. If he is just about to receive it, defenders should try not to give him time to control it. Here, as the ball approaches, the defender stays close. Even if he does not tackle and win the ball, his challenge will have put his opponent off and reduced his freedom of movement.

Tackling practice

One player tries to tackle or intercept while two others pass the ball between them in a small space, about 3 m (or yards) square. Take it in turns to be the tackler and see who gets the ball most.

3 Sliding tackle

The sliding tackle is used in more desperate situations, not so much to gain possession as to get the ball away from the opponent's legs. The tackler approaches from the side, slides in on the leg nearest the opponent and kicks the ball away firmly with his outside foot, as he falls. If the tackler makes contact with his opponent's legs before he touches the ball, it is a foul and his team is penalized, so timing is very important. (See pages 21 and 22 for the relevant laws.) Sliding tackles work best on wet surfaces.

Head down, eyes on ball.

Tackling leg stretches for ball.

Supporting leg bent under body.

4 Timing a tackle

Getting the timing of any tackle exactly right is crucial. In this picture, the defender has tried to tackle too soon and the attacker simply flicks the ball over his outstretched leg.

Improve your heading

Stand about 2 m (or yards) away from another player and count how many times you can head the ball backwards and forwards between you without it touching the ground. Volley if you can't get to the ball with your head.

You can practise heading on your own by throwing a ball against a wall and heading the rebound. Practise taking off from your right and left foot alternately, and remember to keep your eyes open all the time.

Intercepting the ball
In the air

Defenders have to react to danger swiftly. In this picture, number 5 has made no move, but 3 quickly gets in front of the attacker and heads clear. Calling out, for example "Mike's ball", helps to ensure that other defenders do not go for the same ball.

On the ground

Here, the defender has not been able to tackle, but he chases after his opponent and puts out his leg in the hope of intercepting a pass. Even if he fails, he might unsettle the attacker and force him to pass badly.

From a pass

The defender judges the speed of the pass, decides he can stop it reaching number 10 and moves fast along the shortest route to the line of the ball. The safest way to bring a moving ground ball under control is to use the inside of the foot.

9

Defending

1 Marking

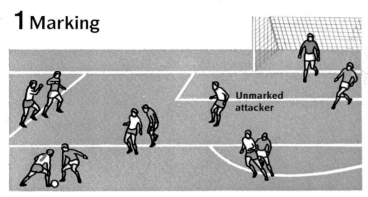

Unmarked attacker

When an attack gets close to the goal, the defending team marks man-to-man, as in this picture. This means that each player follows an opponent wherever he goes. When you are watching a game, notice how close the defenders stay to their opponents and watch out for unmarked attackers. Man-to-man marking is also used at corners, free kicks and sometimes for a whole game.

2

In the zonal marking system, each defender guards an area of the pitch against any attacker who comes into it. This system requires good understanding between the defenders, who must not be lured into opening up gaps by moving too far from their zone. Once an attack is in or near the penalty area, or at a corner or free kick, man-to-man marking is adopted.

3

Sweeper

Sometimes, one of the defenders, known as the sweeper, plays behind the others, "sweeping" up any attackers or loose balls that get through. He does not mark anyone and can run through the line of defenders to play alongside his team's forwards.

4

If a defender gets into difficulty (by making an unsuccessful tackle as in this picture, for example), a team-mate who does not have a zone to guard or a specific opponent to mark should back him up by running in to cover.

Marking practice

A good way of improving your marking is to get someone to run with the ball, changing speed and direction as much as possible, while you try to keep up with them. You can also put a ball on the ground and race for it.

Safety in defence

If defenders are challenged near their own goal, they have to clear the ball from the danger area immediately. A general rule is "play the way you are facing". It may seem negative when a player passes back towards his own goal (and remember, the goalkeeper cannot touch such a pass with his hands) or kicks into touch, but it is safer than trying to dribble or pass upfield under pressure. Here, seeing his goalkeeper is on the ground, a defender kicks the ball over the goal-corner. It is better to give away a corner than a goal.

Jockeying an opponent

Jockeying an opponent, as number 3 is doing here, gives the rest of the defence time to organize themselves. The defender faces the attacker, about 1 m (or yard) away, slowing down his progress and preparing to challenge if he loses control of the ball.

Volleying from defence

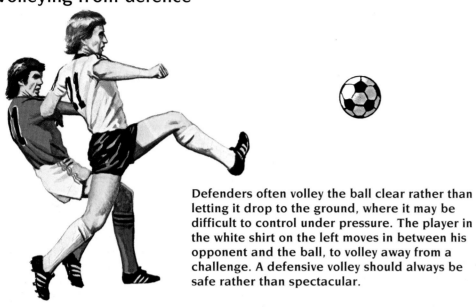

Defenders often volley the ball clear rather than letting it drop to the ground, where it may be difficult to control under pressure. The player in the white shirt on the left moves in between his opponent and the ball, to volley away from a challenge. A defensive volley should always be safe rather than spectacular.

Body contact

The only form of deliberate body contact allowed in soccer is the shoulder charge. In this picture, number 5 is not fouling number 9 in trying to nudge him off the ball. He is using only the top part of his arm against the top part of his opponent's arm. His elbow is safely tucked in and the ball is within playing distance.

You will sometimes see a defender deliberately fouling his opponent in a desperate attempt to win the ball or stop a goal being scored. But this only results in his team being penalized and can cause injury. (For more about the laws on fouls, see pages 21 and 22.)

Forming a wall

When facing a free kick in front of goal, the defending team forms a protective wall of players under the supervision of its goalkeeper. The wall covers one side of the goal and the goalkeeper covers the other. The players in the wall stand shoulder to shoulder, but do not link arms, so that they can break free immediately the kick is taken. Look out for an opponent standing in the wall, attempting to confuse the defence.

Facing a corner

When you are watching a match, notice how the players in the defending team position themselves for a corner. The goalkeeper covers the far post, while a defender (usually the one marking the kicker) covers the near post. Every opponent whether inside the penalty area or waiting outside it, should be tightly marked. Notice, in this picture, how the defenders have positioned themselves goal-side of their opponents.

Positioning

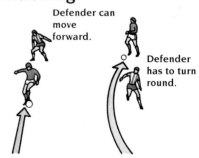

Defender can move forward.

Defender has to turn round.

Whenever possible, a defender positions himself behind his opponent. Then, if the opponent gets the ball, the defender can move forward to get into a position to tackle. If the defender is in front of his opponent and the ball goes past him, he has to turn round before he can challenge.

Goalkeeping

The goalkeeper is probably the most important individual member of a team and one of the most exciting to watch in action. The main responsibility for keeping the ball out of the goal rests with him.

A goalkeeper has to develop different, more specialized skills from the rest of the team, as you can see on these three pages. He needs to have especially quick reactions and good concentration, even when the ball is at the other end of the pitch. As the player with the best overall view of the pitch, he can also help his team-mates by shouting directions.

Catching

1

Body faces flight of ball.

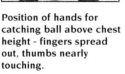

Position of hands for catching ball above chest height - fingers spread out, thumbs nearly touching.

When a goalkeeper jumps to catch a high ball, notice how he tries to face the oncoming direction ("flight") of the ball. After catching it firmly, he immediately brings it down and in to his body for safety. Some goalkeepers wear gloves in wet weather to help stop the ball

Arms and body form cradle for ball.

2

Arms and legs act as shield.

Position of hands for catching ball at chest height or below - fingers spread out, little fingers nearly touching.

When he is gathering a ball which is rolling along the ground, he has to watch for unexpected bounces. He tries to position his arms and legs as

3

Knee across path of ball.

a shield behind the line of the ball, by bending either at the waist (picture 2) or at the knees (picture 3), and he scoops the ball up to his chest.

4

So as not to be pushed off balance by a hard shot coming at his chest or stomach, he has to cushion the impact of the ball. He does this by pulling back the middle of his body slightly, while he catches, as though it were swallowing the ball.

Diving save

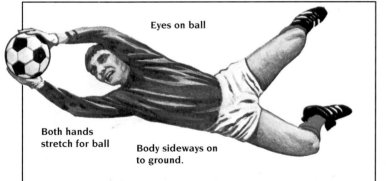

Eyes on ball

Both hands stretch for ball

Body sideways on to ground.

For a diving save, the goalkeeper takes off from one foot (the one nearest the ball) to gain maximum height and power. By facing the ball, not the ground, with the front of his body, he presents as big a wall as possible to it. As soon as he has hold of the ball, he starts to bring it in close to his body, so that attackers have no opportunity to kick it away.

Positioning for a corner

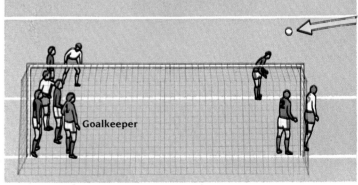

Goalkeeper

It is easier to move forwards than backwards and you will see that, at a corner, the goalkeeper stands at the post furthest away from the ball. This is so he can move forward when the kick is taken, while a defender guards the area behind him. Notice in this picture how the defending players (in the red kit) are forming a rectangle to back up their goalkeeper.

1 Narrowing the angle

Angle is wide.

When a lone attacker breaks through the defence with the ball, the goalkeeper should not stay on the goal-line. If he does, he gives his opponent a very large area of the goal to shoot at, and a good chance of scoring, as you can see here.

2

Angle is narrowed.

By coming off the line towards the attacker, he reduces the shooter's target area and "narrows the angle" he has to shoot from. Timing is crucial. If he comes out too soon, he gives the opponent an opportunity to dribble round him.

3

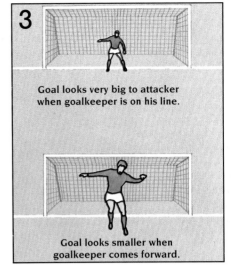

Goal looks very big to attacker when goalkeeper is on his line.

Goal looks smaller when goalkeeper comes forward.

Smothering

Sometimes, the only way of saving a goal is for the goalkeeper to dive right at an attacker's feet and smother the ball with his body. He makes sure his body is sideways on to the ground and curls round the ball. Timing is very important. If he dives only a moment too soon, the attacker can kick the ball over his body. A moment too late and it can slip under him.

Punching

Ball punched in middle.

Fists clenched like this.

If the ball is too high to catch or opponents are crowding him, the goalkeeper may have to punch the ball clear. He punches as hard as he can, if possible using both fists clenched to send the ball back in the direction from which it came.

Deflecting

If the ball is very close to the goal and neither catching nor punching is possible, the goalkeeper can use the palm or fingers of his hand to tip it over the bar or round the post. He has to be careful that the ball does not rebound off the post or bar, back into play.

Test your reflexes

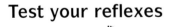

Stand with your back to another player, about 4 m (or yards) away. Get him to kick a ball at you, calling out as he does so. When you hear the call, turn and try to save. You could use several balls in succession to see how many times you can save the shot.

Sit on the ground 2-3 m (or yards) from another player, who throws the ball at varying heights towards an imaginary goal behind you. As the ball leaves his hands, get up and try to save. Count how many goals you can stop. Practise in front of a real goal if you can.

13

Stopping ground shots

Low shots near the body are difficult for goalkeepers to save. You will often see inexperienced goalkeepers diving right over them and letting the ball slip underneath their body. Here is a good example of how it should be done. The goalkeeper just drops on to the ball, keeping his legs well out of the way, so that his hands and the upper part of his body can bring the ball to safety.

Kicking

When he wants to get the ball back into the other team's half of the pitch, the goalkeeper usually kicks it. If he has enough space, he can volley the ball from his hand. This sort of kick is called a "punt" or "drop kick".

Ball held well forward.

Kicking leg straightens from hip.

Ball kicked with instep for power.

Follow-through in direction of target.

Throwing

When he has possession of the ball, the goalkeeper must "distribute" it (give it back to his team-mates) as quickly as possible, so they can start a counter-attack. The safest way of distributing the ball is to throw it, although he cannot do this if the ball has been passed back to him by a teammate. You will see goalkeepers using three main types of throw.

If there is an unmarked team-mate nearby, the goalkeeper can roll the ball to him underarm, along the ground.

An accurate overarm throw can catch the opposition off guard, if it is made quickly, and as hard and low as possible, so they cannot easily intercept. The power comes from the shoulder, with a flick of the wrist as the ball is released, and a strong follow-through.

A throw similar to bowling a cricket ball will go further, but is not as accurate as the short throw from the shoulder. Watch for the throwing arm swinging up in an arc, while the other arm swings down. Both arms are kept straight, right up to the moment the ball is released.

Tactics

Before each game the manager, coach and team meet to discuss tactics. They decide what position each of the players will play in, which formation (see right) they will use and which opposition player each of them will mark when defending. (For more about marking, see page 10.) Below are just a few of the things that have to be taken into account when tactics are being decided and a team selected.

1 Conditions

Some players play better than others in certain conditions. For example, small players usually keep their footing better on slippery or icy surfaces. Strength is needed to keep running on a very muddy pitch. Players who are not at peak fitness may not perform well in extreme heat.

2 Opposition

It is useful to have some idea of how the opposition team normally plays and the strengths and weaknesses of its players. For example, an inexperienced defender may not be capable of marking a clever winger and a small centre forward may have to keep passing back to avoid being challenged by a tall, opposing centre back. If one of the opposition is particularly skilful, a defender might be detailed to mark him throughout the game.

3 Game and venue

A team does not always need to win a match. Sometimes a draw is enough. For example, if they only need one point to win a league. In this case they may decide to adopt defensive tactics. When competitions are played in two legs, such as the European Cup, teams often prefer to play attacking soccer in the home leg, when they are familiar with the ground, and more defensively in the away leg. (You can find out how different sorts of soccer competition are organized on pages 30-31.)

4 Players

If a regular player is injured, the tactics may have to be changed to suit the players who are available.

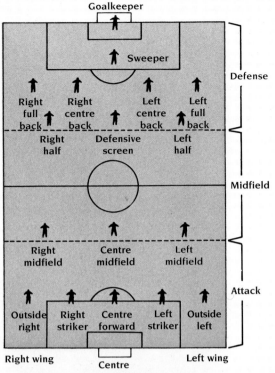

Positions and formations

A team places its 11 players in any of the 17 positions shown in the diagram on the left. You will rarely see a team playing with more than four attackers, even more rarely with more than one winger.

The choice of formation depends on all the things listed in the left-hand column of this page, but it always has to be suited to the individual players in the team. It is especially important for the defensive part of a formation to be well organized. Attacks can afford to rely rather more on spontaneity and imagination. All the systems shown below are flexible enough to allow players to improvise, depending on the state of the game.

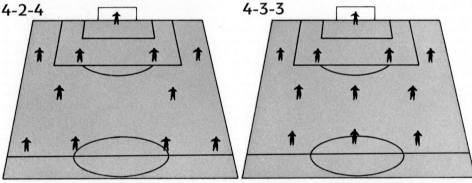

4-2-4

The success of this formation depends on the ability of the two midfielders to link up with both attackers and defenders. It is possible to have six players attacking or six defending, but the midfielders' stamina is crucial

4-3-3

Here, there are only three attackers, so the midfielders or full backs have to come forward and overlap to give the attack width. This is a hard system for the attackers because they usually have to face four opposing defenders.

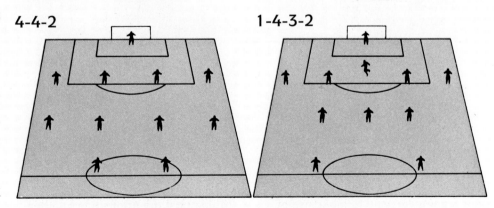

4-4-2

This is a more defensive formation. Eight men can be called upon for defence, but there is great pressure on the two strikers to keep the ball until midfielders can help them in attack.

1-4-3-2

The most heavily defensive system is the one in which there is a sweeper (see page 10) and the rest of the team mark opponents man-to-man. Sometimes the sweeper plays in front of the defence, acting as a screen.

Teamwork

Tactics can only succeed if every player understands his role within the agreed system and is prepared to play accordingly. Eleven players working as a unit, backing each other up and adjusting their positions in relation to each other as well as to the ball, are far more effective than 11 brilliant individuals all trying to show off their personal talent.

The captain acts as leader of the team and as the coach's representative on the pitch. He gives instructions to his team-mates, provides encouragement, and tries to set a good example.

Teamwork takes time and training to develop. Here are some ways in which players can contribute to successful team-play

Set pieces

Set pieces are routines which a team works out in advance and rehearses in training for use at throw-ins, corners and free kicks. Sometimes it is decided before the match who will play what role in a set piece. As the occasion arises, sometimes the players organize themselves on the pitch. Here is an example of a set piece at a throw-in. Look out for similar ones when you are watching a match.

Players always have to be aware of where their team-mates are. As number 10 receives the ball, he has to glance up to check that number 8 is running into position, ready to shoot, as rehearsed in training.

As the ball is thrown in, two attackers (numbers 7 and 10) confuse their markers by running across their line of vision. The markers would have expected number 7 to receive the ball - instead, number 10 takes it.

"Running off the ball" (this means running without the ball) is an essential part of teamwork, even when it is running with no intention of receiving a pass. Here, 9 and 11 run away from the goal to make space for 8, and to confuse the defence.

Playing to strengths

Players need to know the strengths of their team-mates and to make use of them whenever possible.

Here, the player in possession has time and room to consider his next move. The three team-mates nearest him are all closely marked, so it is dangerous to pass to them. He is not covered by a team-mate, so if he tries to dribble past the opposition number 8 and fails, number 8 will have a clear run down the wing. His number 9 is much smaller than the opponent marking him, so a long ball in the air might be wasted. He could pass to 6, or back to the goalkeeper, but the team wants to play fast, attacking soccer, so he would prefer to pass forward. He knows his number 8 is a quick runner and so decides to play a long, fast ball into a space for him. Meanwhile, on the far side of the pitch, 11 prepares to run forward to support the attack.

he offside trap

Trap moves forward and makes player receiving ball offside.

Trap moves too late, receiver delays his run and is not offside when ball is played.

A common example of teamwork is the use of the offside trap. To spot the trap in operation at a match, you need to understand the offside law (see page 23). The aim of the trap is for defenders deliberately to force an opposing attacker offside. They rush forward in unison towards the half-way line, so that there is only the goalkeeper left between the attacker and the goal at the moment the ball is played. This is often criticized as a negative tactic, but an alert forward line can beat the trap with well-timed runs.

Communicating on the pitch

In a crowded stadium you cannot hear players constantly shouting to each other, but successful teamwork depends very much on calling out and signalling. Pre-arranged signals are often used at set pieces to indicate which routine the thrower or kicker is going to try. Here are some of the calls players give, and their meanings. Players should always give the name of the person they are shouting to, if there is any risk of confusing the opposition.

MAN ON!

Opponent approaching from behind.

HOLD!

Help is on its way from an overlapper.

MARK UP!

CENTRE!

Goalkeeper tells team-mates to mark opponents.

Unmarked attacker calls for ball.

There is an unmarked attacker in centre of pitch.

TACKLE!

Cover is available, so player can tackle instead of jockeying.

Slowing down the game

Foot on ball

This is a legitimate tactic, as it is time-consuming, not time-wasting, for instance to allow strikers to move upfield or give defenders a breathing space after a burst of fast play. If the goalkeeper holds on to the ball for a lengthy period, though, the team will be penalized for time-wasting.

Team-play practice

Play a game in which no one is allowed to touch the ball more than once before another player makes contact. This is good practice for running off the ball and helping out team-mates. Have up to five players a side.

Super skills

All players have to master the basic skills of soccer, but there are additional skills and tricks which can transform a game within seconds. Top professionals spend hours perfecting these and many develop their own individual tricks which make them instantly recognizable on the pitch. Here are some super skills for you to look out for in matches.

Body feint

1

Attacker moves away from ball.

Attacker spins round, collects ball and moves off.

2

Opponent automatically follows.

You will sometimes see a player break free of an opponent who is jockeying him, by moving suddenly to one side without the ball. Then, as the opponent starts to follow, the player quickly turns and moves off in the opposite direction, with the ball. This is a dangerous trick to try if the opponent is less than a 1 m (1 yd) away and could intercept.

Drag back

Sole of right foot drags ball back from opponent.

Player pivots and transfers weight to right foot.

Skilful players often use the front of their sole to drag the ball back from an opponent's challenge. In these pictures, the player in possession tempts the challenger to go for the ball, then drags it back with the sole of his right foot as the tackle comes in. As soon as the ball is clear, he pivots on his left foot, transfers his weight to his right foot and takes the ball away with his left foot.

Swerving the ball

1

Swerving the ball with the inside of the foot, often called a "banana kick", is much more difficult than swerving it with the outside (see page 7). Only very skilful players can curve the ball round an opponent or defensive wall.

2

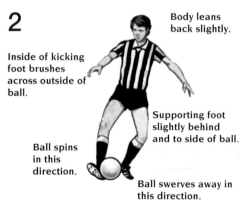

Body leans back slightly.

Inside of kicking foot brushes across outside of ball.

Supporting foot slightly behind and to side of ball.

Ball spins in this direction.

Ball swerves away in this direction.

The supporting foot is placed slightly behind and to the side of the ball. The front of the inside of the kicking foot brushes firmly across the outside of the ball. The lower down the ball is struck, the higher it rises.

Back-heeling

When a player can see no way past an opponent, you will sometimes see him kicking the ball backwards to a team-mate with his heel. This is a dangerous move for a player to try too close to his own goal, but a good call will tell him if a back-heel is safe.

Long throw-in

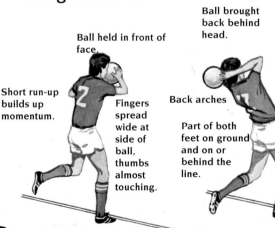

Short run-up builds up momentum.

Ball held in front of face.

Fingers spread wide at side of ball, thumbs almost touching.

Ball brought back behind head.

Back arches

Part of both feet on ground and on or behind the line.

Knees bent to give mobility at waist.

One foot in front of other to give extra power.

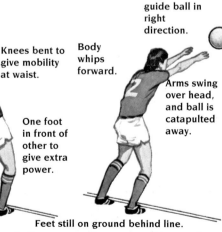

Body whips forward.

Fingers guide ball in right direction.

Arms swing over head, and ball is catapulted away.

Feet still on ground behind line.

A long throw-in can be as threatening to defenders as a corner kick. Good throwers can get the ball from the touch-line, near the corner flag, as far as the goal-mouth. For the law about throw-ins, see page 22.

Bicycle kick

Eyes on ball

One-footed take-off from non-kicking foot.

Non-kicking leg thrust up from hip.

Top half of body arches backwards.

Toes pointed.

Kicking leg swings up and non-kicking leg swings down in scissors motion.

Ball struck with instep.

Arms out, fingers spread, to break fall.

This is one of the most spectacular soccer kicks, sometimes used by defenders to clear the ball from their area but more often by strikers attempting to score when they have their back to the opposition goal. The referee might consider the bicycle kick to be dangerous play if it is made too near other players.

Turning on the ball

When a striker receives the ball and needs to change direction, you might see him "turn on the ball", especially if there is no team-mate nearby for him to pass to. This means that he turns to face the goal, at the same time as he brings the ball under control. Here is an example.

Leg curls round ball.

Body between ball and defender, in line with flight of ball.

Eyes on ball

Supporting leg pivots to push player away in direction of goal.

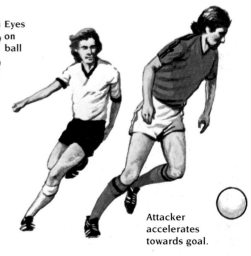

Attacker accelerates towards goal.

Turning on the ball race

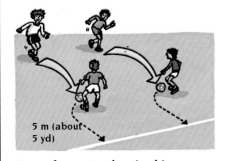

5 m (about 5 yd)

Four of you stand as in this picture. The two with their backs to the line are fed passes along the ground by the other two. As you bring the ball under control, turn and race for the line. Have ten goes and see who wins most.

Laying the ball off

A striker often receives the ball with his back to the opponents' goal. If he is closely marked, as in this picture, he might "lay the ball off" (pass it back) to an unmarked team-mate. Then he can turn and run forward to receive another pass.

Dummy

Look out for players jumping over the ball to fool or "dummy" an opponent, especially at set pieces. Here, a defender moves in to tackle number 9, but the pass goes on to another attacker. This trick requires good calling between team-mates.

Soccer laws

The pitch

A soccer pitch must be 90-120 m (100-130 yd) long and 45-90 m (50-100 yd) wide. Though a pitch for an international match must be 100-110 m long (110-120 yd) and 64-75 m (70-80 yd) wide. The touch line must always be longer than the goal line.

All metric figures here are the official FIFA conversions.

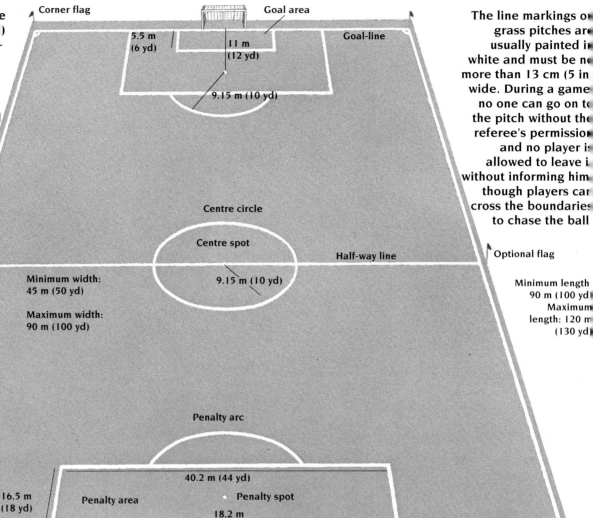

- Corner flag
- Goal area
- 5.5 m (6 yd)
- 11 m (12 yd)
- Goal-line
- 9.15 m (10 yd)
- Centre circle
- Centre spot
- Touch-line
- Half-way line
- 9.15 m (10 yd)
- Optional flag
- Minimum width: 45 m (50 yd)
- Maximum width: 90 m (100 yd)
- Minimum length 90 m (100 yd) Maximum length: 120 m (130 yd)
- Penalty arc
- 40.2 m (44 yd)
- Penalty spot
- 16.5 m (18 yd)
- Penalty area
- 18.2 m (20 yd)
- 1 m (1 yd)
- 11 m (12 yd)
- 5.5 m (6 yd)
- Goal 7.32 m (8 yd)
- 2.4 m (8 ft)
- 16.5 m (18 yd)

The line markings on grass pitches are usually painted in white and must be no more than 13 cm (5 in) wide. During a game no one can go on to the pitch without the referee's permission and no player is allowed to leave it without informing him, though players can cross the boundaries to chase the ball.

The ball

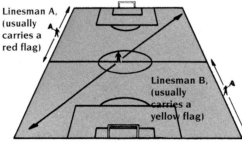

A soccer ball is made of leather or a synthetic alternative and measures 68.5-71 cm (27-28 in) in circumference. At the beginning of a match, it has to weigh 396-453 gm (14-16 oz) and be inflated to a pressure of 600-1,100 gm/cm^2 (8.5-15.6 pounds per square inch). It can be any colour.

The officials

- Linesman A, (usually carries a red flag)
- Linesman B, (usually carries a yellow flag)

So that they can follow the game as closely as possible, the two linesmen watch one half of the pitch each and the referee works on a diagonal line, covering the parts of the pitch which are furthest from both of them. The referee always has the final decision.

Check-list of officials' duties

Before kick-off the officials check:
1 The pitch, including the markings. If the referee thinks the pitch is dangerous (e.g. if it is icy or too wet), he can call off the match.
2 The goals. The ball can slip through a loosely secured net, making it hard to tell if a goal has been scored.
3 Players' equipment. Nothing must be worn which might injure another player, e.g. boots with dangerous studs, or jewellery. Shinguards are compulsory.
4 The ball. For an important match the referee may have to choose from a selection of balls.
5 Team lists. In some competitions each team has to say who is playing and at what number, and who the substitutes are.

Kick-off

9.15 m (10 yd)

Ball on centre spot.

A coin is tossed to decide which team kicks off. Players stand in their own half, with the opposition outside the centre circle. The ball must be kicked forward. A goal cannot be scored direct from a kick-off. After a goal is scored, the non-scoring side kicks off.

Timekeeping

Referee blows whistle and signals for end of half

Linesman's signal for end of half.

Both the referee and the linesman carry stop-watches and keep time: 45 minutes for each half of the match. The referee also keeps a note of any time to be added on to each half for injuries or other stoppages. There is usually break at half time of at least five minutes.

Advantage

Referee waves play on.

If a player is fouled, the referee usually stops play, but if the fouled player or his team keeps possession, and a stoppage might benefit the offender's team (by giving it time to organize its defence, for example), he may allow play to continue.

Drop ball

After a stoppage which was not caused by an infringement of the law (injury, for example), the referee restarts play by dropping the ball, at the spot where it was last played. The players are not allowed to kick the ball until it touches the ground.

Substitution

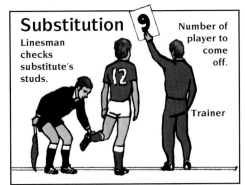

Linesman checks substitute's studs.

Number of player to come off.

Trainer

One or two substitutes are allowed in most competitions. A substitute is only allowed to go on to the pitch during a stoppage in the game and only at a signal from the referee. Once a player has been taken off and substituted, he is not allowed to rejoin the game.

Discipline

For persistent infringements of the law, arguing with officials, or behaving irresponsibly, the referee can caution or "book" a player. You will see him writing the player's name in a notebook and showing him a yellow card.

Ball out of play

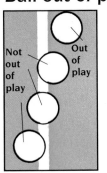

Not out of play

Out of play

Out of play

The ball is out of play when the whole of it crosses the touch-line or the goal-line, either on the ground or in the air. If the ball curves back on to the pitch after once going over the line, it is still considered out of play.

Goal

Goal

No goal

Goal

For a goal to be scored, the whole of the ball must cross the goal-line between the posts and under the bar. If a goalkeeper stops a ball when he is on, or in front of, the goal-line, but the whole of the ball is behind it, then a goal is scored.

For more major offences, such as serious foulplay, or foul or abusive language or misbehaving after a caution, a player may be sent off. He cannot return or be substituted. Look out for a red card, which indicates a sending-off.

Free kicks

When a player infringes the law, the other team is awarded a free kick from the spot where the offence took place.

The player taking the kick must wait for the referee's signal before he kicks. The ball must be stationary and no opponent is allowed within 9.15 m (10 yd) of the ball. (The exception is when an indirect free kick is given less than 9.15 m (10 yd) from the goal. Then, the defending team can stand on their goal-line between the goal-posts.)

There are two types of free kick: direct and indirect. A goal can be scored from a direct free kick, but after an indirect free kick at least one other player must touch the ball before a goal can be scored.

Signal for indirect free kick.

Signal for direct free kick.

Indirect free kicks

These are awarded for dangerous play (for example, raising the feet too high), charging a player when he is not in possession of the ball, charging the goalkeeper when he is not in possession of the ball, and, in the case of the goalkeeper, taking more than four steps while handling the ball. Time-wasting may also be penalized with an indirect free kick.

Direct free kicks

These are awarded for kicking or attempting to kick an opponent, tripping him, jumping at him, charging him dangerously, hitting or attempting to hit him, holding him, pushing him and for intentionally handling the ball.

When you are watching a match, see how quickly you can spot the offences for which free kicks are given.

Penalty kicks

If a player commits an offence for which a direct free kick is normally awarded in his own team's penalty area, the opposition is awarded a penalty kick. A goal can be scored direct from a penalty kick.

If the defending team breaks any of the rules (see the picture on the right) and a goal is not scored, the kick is retaken.

If the kicker breaks any of the rules, the opposition is awarded an indirect free kick.

If any other member of the attacking team breaks the rules and a goal is scored, the goal is not allowed and the kick is retaken.

If a penalty is awarded close to the end of half or full time, extra time is added on for it to be taken.

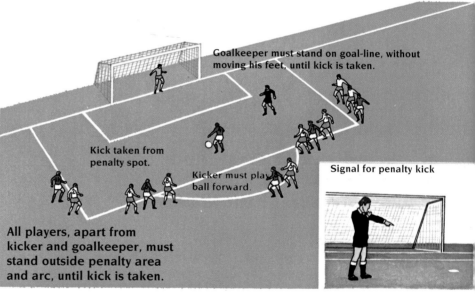

Goalkeeper must stand on goal-line, without moving his feet, until kick is taken.

Kick taken from penalty spot.

Kicker must play ball forward.

Signal for penalty kick

All players, apart from kicker and goalkeeper, must stand outside penalty area and arc, until kick is taken.

Restarts

Throw-ins

Ball must be thrown with both hands from behind and over head.

Part of both feet must be on ground, either on or behind touch-line.

Signal for throw-in to team playing in direction of flag.

If the ball goes out of play over the touch-line, a throw-in is given to the team which was not the last to touch the ball. It must be taken at the point where the ball crossed the line. A goal cannot be scored direct from a throw-in.

Corner kicks

Defenders at least 9.15 m (10 yd) away.

Signal for corner kick.

When a member of the defending team puts the ball out of play over the goal-line, a corner kick is awarded to the attacking team. The kick is taken at the corner on the side of the pitch the ball went out of play. A goal can be scored direct.

The offside rule

The aim of the offside law is to stop forwards loitering around their opponents' goal, waiting for a chance to score without playing a full part in the game.

A player is offside if he is nearer the opposition's goal-line than the ball, at the exact moment the ball was last touched, unless:

1 The last person to play the ball was an opposition player.
2 He is not nearer* to his opponents' goal-line than at least two of his opponents.

3 He is in his own half of the pitch.
4 He receives the ball direct from a throw-in, goal kick, corner kick or drop ball.

The penalty for being offside is an indirect free kick to the other team.

You will often see a team deliberately try to make an opposition attacker offside by using a tactic known as the "offside trap". To find out how the trap works, see page 17.

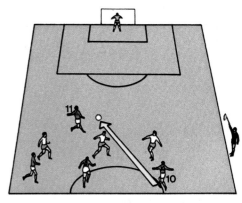

Offside. Number 11 is nearer the opposition's goal than the ball is at the moment that number 10 passes to him and there is only one opposition player (the goalkeeper) between him and the goal-line.

Linesman's signal for offside.

Player on far side of pitch.

Player in middle of pitch.

Player on near side of pitch.

Immediately an official sees a player is offside, he must decide if he is influencing play to his team's advantage. If he is running back into position or is injured, he might not be signalled offside.

The offside law is the most difficult soccer rule to understand and enforce correctly, and it is sometimes difficult for a player to know if he is offside. The

officials' verdict may sometimes be unpopular, but their decision is always final.

Try paying attention to the offside law when you are watching a match. See if you can spot offside players as quickly as the officials do. Look out for the linesmen's signals telling the referee what part of the pitch the offside player is in.

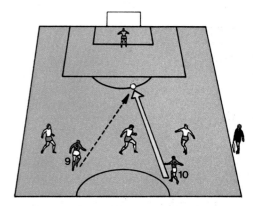

Not offside. Number 9 has four opponents between him and the goal-line at the moment number 10 plays the ball forward. He can legitimately run into the space to collect the pass.

Goal kicks

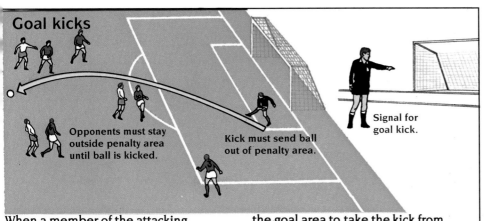

Opponents must stay outside penalty area until ball is kicked.

Kick must send ball out of penalty area.

Signal for goal kick.

When a member of the attacking team puts the ball out of play over the goal-line, a goal kick is awarded to the defending team. The goalkeeper can choose which side of

the goal area to take the kick from. A goal cannot be scored direct. Goal kicks are usually, though not necessarily, taken by the goalkeeper.

Not offside. Number 9 looks offside, but the last person to play the ball was an opponent, number 7. He has made a bad pass into a space where there is no team-mate to receive it.

*He is onside if he is level with two opponents.

Improve your soccer

There are many different games you can play based on soccer, all of which help to improve the skills you need for a full 11-a-side game.

Some of the games described on these two pages are useful because you only need a few players and not much space to play them. Each game, or practice, is specially good for developing the skills which are shown in brackets after their names.

Juggling (ball control)

Throw the ball up gently in front of you and then try and keep it off the ground, using your instep, the top of your thigh and your forehead. This is more difficult than clever players make it look, so don't get discouraged. Use your arms to steady you and don't try to make the ball go high. Aim to make five "touches" to start with and build up the number gradually. At first you might find it easier to make the touches against a wall. You can also practise juggling with a friend and see who can keep the ball in the air the longest.

Tennis ball (heading and volleying)

For this game you need between three and six players a side. It is often played on badminton or volley-ball courts, but you can mark out your own court outdoors. Rig up a net, or make do with a piece of string or washing line tied between strong posts, trees or walls, at about chest height.

A player puts the ball into play, or "serves", by throwing or kicking it from the back line of his team's half of the court over the net into the other team's half. The ball is then headed or volleyed backwards and forwards across the net. Up to three passes are allowed between team-mates before sending the ball over. A team only wins a point if it is serving. So, when a player lets the ball touch the ground, or sends it out of court, or when it is passed more than three times between team-mates, the other team wins the serve and, if it was last to serve, also gets a point. Play to 15 points.

Wall ball (kicking and control)

Any number up to six can play. You kick the ball against a wall in an agreed order and are only allowed to touch it once at each go.

If your kick does not reach the wall with one touch, you lose a life. If you lose three lives, you are out of the game.

Shoot-out (shooting and saving)

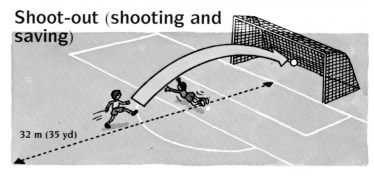

32 m (35 yd)

Each team takes it in turn to have one player try to shoot past the goalkeeper. He starts 32 m (35 yd) from the goal and must shoot within 5 seconds. If, after five members of each team have had a shot, the scores are still equal, other players continue the shoot-out until one team goes ahead with an equal number of kicks taken. If you want to practise shooting like this, start off about 25 paces away from the goal.

Five-a-side soccer (control and teamwork)

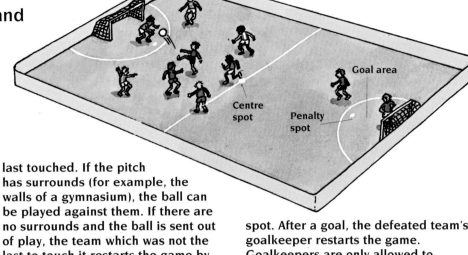

Five-a-side soccer is played both outdoors and indoors and the size of the pitch varies. You may find you can play at a local sports centre.

Each team has a goalkeeper and four other players. Only the goalkeeper is allowed in the goal area. If a member of the attacking team goes in, a free kick is given to the defending team. If a member of the defending team goes in, a penalty is awarded to the attackers. If a player goes into the area by mistake and is not affecting the game, he is not penalized.

The ball is not allowed to go above shoulder height. If it does, the team which was not the last to touch it gets a free kick from the spot where it was last touched. If the pitch has surrounds (for example, the walls of a gymnasium), the ball can be played against them. If there are no surrounds and the ball is sent out of play, the team which was not the last to touch it restarts the game by kicking it back on to the pitch from the spot where it went out.

There is no offside rule and charging is forbidden. The game is started by a drop ball on the centre spot. After a goal, the defeated team's goalkeeper restarts the game. Goalkeepers are only allowed to distribute the ball by rolling it underarm. A game is usually played for six minutes each half.

All other rules are the same as for 11-a-side soccer (see pages 20-23).

Target practice (accuracy)

Chalk a goal on a wall as shown in this picture to practise shooting. Start off by aiming for box 1. If you hit it, try for box 2, then for box 3, and so on. When you miss your target, it is the other person's turn. Every time you get a turn, you aim for the box you missed last shot. The first to get to 8 is the winner. You can also practise this on your own, moving back as you improve and shooting from different angles.

About 2 m (or yards)

Set up objects (cricket stumps, garden canes, a pile of stones) in the distance and aim to hit them or pass the ball between them.

Try chipping a ball (see page 2) into a bucket about 5 m (or yards) away from you. Move further back as you improve.

Four-goal soccer (shooting, positioning and defending)

You can play this in one half of a normal soccer pitch and to the normal soccer rules (see pages 20-23). The difference is that each team has two goals, placed on the touch-lines, and the goalkeeper has to protect both of them. It is best to play with a minimum of five and a maximum of seven a side.

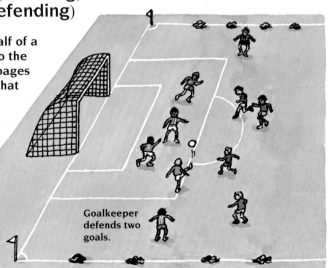

Goalkeeper defends two goals.

Other ideas to try

1 In an ordinary game, make it a rule that every player has to beat an opponent before passing. This improves dribbling and tackling.

2 Play with uneven teams, e.g. four against five. This gives one team lots of scoring opportunities and the other practice in defence.

3 If there are no more than about six players in a side, pass to one another in an agreed order. If the order is broken without the other side intercepting, they get a free kick. This is good for control, running off the ball and passing.

Training and fitness

Professional soccer players train for about two hours every day, except on match days and the day after. Their training time is spent improving the ball skills shown earlier in this book, developing teamwork and, very important, keeping fit.

On this page are some of the professionals' fitness routines for you to try. Remember that you can only get fit gradually and don't overstrain yourself. If you are not already fit, the exercises will make you tired, but if you start to feel really exhausted, stop and have a rest. Remember not to exercise too soon after having a meal.

Warming up

Always warm up your muscles for 5-10 minutes before you start training or playing a match. Watch how a team exercises on the pitch before a match and notice how the players try to get a feel of the ball with simple passing routines.

Body and supporting leg straight.

Bend knee up to chest.

Arms by sides

Legs straight, touch toes.

Body straight

Bend front leg

Hands on hips

Back leg straight

Front foot faces forward.

Back foot at right angles to body.

Arm stretched

Knees straight

Legs apart

Touch opposite ankle with hand.

Sprints

Jumping

Keeping your feet flat on the ground, stretch up and make a mark as high as you can on a wall, with a piece of chalk. Turn sideways to the wall, jump and make another mark as high as you can. Measure the difference between the two. Scores: 20 cm (8 in) - poor; 45 cm (18 in) - good; 60 cm (24 in) - excellent.

Sit or lie on the ground and at a shout from a friend scramble up and jump as high as you can, facing the way they tell you: left, right, forward or back.

Jump on and off a low wall, bench or step about 20 times. Gradually increase the number of jumps you do.

Stamina

8 paces

Put five markers on the ground, about eight paces apart. Sprint round the first one and back to the start. Then, without stopping, round the second and back, and so on. You should be able to get round all five in a minute. Rest for 45 seconds, then start again. At first, try doing three complete runs in a session and gradually build up to six.

Circuits

Circuits are used to incorporate different aspects of training in the same training session. Here are two ways of using a circuit for building up your fitness.

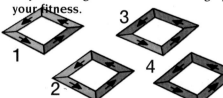

Mark out a square measuring about 20 paces and try and do the complete circuit (numbers 1-4 shown above) twice without stopping. Red arrows mean run, blue arrows mean walk. You can make this exercise into a race by doing it with a friend.

Using the same square, do ten of the exercises shown below at each corner. Jog from corner to corner between the exercises, and don't rush them.

Standing jumps. Keeping the top part of your body straight, arms by your sides, jump as high as you can, bringing your knees up to your chest.

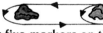

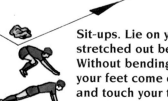

Press-ups. Lie face down, palms beneath your shoulders. Use your hands to push your body up. Your head and shoulders should be in a straight line. Lower your body again but don't let it touch the ground.

Squat thrusts. Crouch on all fours and, keeping your hands in position, jump your feet backwards and forwards.

Sit-ups. Lie on your back, arms stretched out behind your head. Without bending your knees or letting your feet come off the ground, sit up and touch your toes.

Skills to spot

It can be difficult to see exactly what players are doing when a match is moving very fast and parts of the pitch are crowded. The sequences on the next three pages will help you to spot some of the skills which are commonly used and which have been described earlier in this book.

A pass with the inside of the foot

A long high pass

Swerving the ball with the outside of the foot

Volleying a high ball

A half-volley

Back-heeling

Trapping with the instep

Heading to the side

A diving header

Feinting with the foot

Stopping on the ball

Screening the ball

Controlling and turning on the ball

A front block tackle

Attacker
forced off
the ball.

A sliding tackle

Saving a high shot

Saving a low shot

A long overarm throw

Narrowing the angle and smothering

Soccer competitions

How a league is organized

A league is made up of a number of teams who arrange to play each other at least twice during a season, once at home, once away. Points are awarded for a win and for a draw (the exact number varies from league to league) and a team's position in the league depends on the number of points it wins.

When two teams have the same number of points, the one with the better "goal difference" (total number of goals scored minus total number of goals conceded) is placed higher. In the event of goal difference being equal, the team with the higher number of goals scored is placed higher.

League tables

Below is an example of a league table such as you might see on television or in a newspaper, showing how each team stands after five games. This league has four teams. Two points are awarded for a win and one for a draw.

P = Number of games played.
W = Number of games won.
D = Number of games drawn.
L = Number of games lost.
F = (For) Number of goals scored.
A = (Against) Number of goals conceded.
P = Number of points.

	P	W	D	L	F	A	P	Goal difference
Blues	5	3	2	0	11	6	8	+5
Reds	5	2	2	1	10	7	6	+3
Greens	5	1	1	3	8	10	3	-2
Whites	5	1	1	3	5	11	3	-6

Here, the Blues have been awarded two points for each of their three wins, making six points, plus one point for each of their two draws, so they have eight in all. During the course of their five games, they have scored eleven goals, but other teams have scored six against them, so their goal difference is eleven minus six, making five.

See if you can work out what the final positions in the league would be if, in the two remaining games, the scores were: Whites 2, Blues 1; Reds 5, Greens 1. The answer is at the foot of this column.

League divisions

The teams in a league often play in separate "divisions". The team which finishes the season at the top of the highest division wins the league championship. The teams coming highest in lower divisions, usually in the top two or three places, go up or are "promoted" to the next division up. Those finishing the season in the bottom two or three places go down or are "relegated" to the next division down. Teams at the bottom of the lowest division are either replaced by new teams or are voted by other teams to continue in the league.

The final league table would look like this:

	P	W	D	L	F	A	P	Goal difference
Reds	6	3	2	1	15	8	8	+7
Blues	6	3	2	1	12	8	8	+4
Whites	6	2	1	3	7	12	5	-5
Greens	6	1	1	4	9	15	3	-6

How a cup competition is run

There are three main sorts of cup competition.

1 In a straightforward knock-out competition, each team entering is picked at random from a draw to play against one of the other teams. The winners of each game go forward into the next round, where they are again drawn to play one of the other winners. Eventually, only two teams remain to play each other in the final. If a match finishes in a draw, a replay takes place. The English Football Association Cup is organized like this.

2 In two-legged competitions, such as the European cups (see opposite page), teams are drawn to play each other in the same way as for a knock-out competition, but they play each other twice in each round, once at home, once away. The team which has the highest "goal aggregate" (has scored the most goals in the two matches) wins. If the scores are equal, the team which scored the most goals away from home wins because in this case, away goals count double. If these scores are also equal, the teams take it in turns to take penalties against the opposition goalkeeper, until one team has scored more than the other. Each team takes at least five penalties.

3 Some competitions, for example, the World Cup, are organized on a regional basis at the beginning, with each team playing in an area league on a points system. The winners of each league qualify for the finals tournament, where they again play in leagues. The winners of these then play on a knock-out basis until only two teams remain for the final match.

Some competitions are organized using a combination of these three basic methods.

FIFA

The Fédération Internationale de Football Association (FIFA) is the world organization which governs soccer in over 140 countries. It was formed in 1904 and has its headquarters in Zurich, Switzerland. It is divided into six regions, with each region organizing its own competitions between countries and clubs. The regions are:
UEFA (European Union of Football Associations)
Conmebol (South America)
Concacaf (Central and North America, the Caribbean)
Asia
Africa
Oceania (Australasia and the Pacific)

The World Cup

The World Cup is the largest and most important international soccer competition. It is held every four years and is open to all the member nations of FIFA. The competition begins with qualifying rounds played in each FIFA region over a period of two years and ends with a finals tournament held in one country. The current World Cup holders and the country chosen to host the finals are exempt from playing in the qualifying rounds.

Here is a list of the World Cup final winners, since the competition began. The venue is in brackets.
1930   (Uruguay) Uruguay beat Argentina 4-2.
1934   (Italy) Italy beat Czechoslovakia 2-1.
1938   (France) Italy beat Hungary 4-2.
1942   No competition
1946   No competition
1950   (Brazil) Uruguay won the "finalists' league" which temporarily replaced the knock-out system.
1954   (Switzerland) West Germany beat Hungary 3-2.
1958   (Sweden) Brazil beat Sweden 5-2.
1962   (Chile) Brazil beat Czechoslovakia 3-1.
1966   (England) England beat West Germany 4-2.
1970   (Mexico) Brazil beat Italy 4-1.
1974   (West Germany) West Germany beat Holland 2-1.
1978   (Argentina) Argentina beat Holland 3-1.
1982   (Spain) Italy beat West Germany 3-1.
1986   (Mexico) Argentina beat West Germany 3-2.
1990   (Italy) West Germany beat Argentina 1-0.

World Cup facts

In 1994 the World Cup finals are to be held in the USA.

Brazil is the only country to have reached the finals tournament of all competitions.

Brazil and Italy have each won the World Cup three times.

The top scorer in any one finals tournament is the French striker, Just Fontaine, who scored 13 goals in six games in 1958.

The player to score most goals in a final (the game to decide the winners) is Geoff Hurst, who scored three for England in 1966.

The player to appear in the most finals tournaments is Antonio Carbajal, Mexico's goalie in the five tournaments from 1950 to 1966.

The highest World Cup score was in a qualifying round before the finals tournament, when New Zealand beat Fiji 13-0 in 1981.

The original trophy was called the Jules Rimet Cup, after the French president of FIFA in 1930. This trophy was given to the Brazilians after they had won it for the third time in 1970. The new trophy is called the FIFA World Cup.

Other international competitions

The European Championships is held, like the World Cup, every four years, with the qualifying games starting two years before the finals tournament. The competition was first held in 1960 and has been won by Russia, Spain, Italy, Czechoslovakia, France, the Netherlands and West Germany (twice).

The South American Championship takes place at irregular intervals of 1-4 years. Since it was first held in 1916, there have been 34 competitions. Uruguay have won 13 times.

The Central American Championship has been held every 2-4 years since 1941. It has been dominated by Costa Rica, who have won nine times.

The African Nations' Cup has been held every two years since 1957. Ghana have won three times. Algeria were winners in 1989.

The Asian Cup has been held every four years since 1956 and Iran have won three times.

International club competitions

Individual clubs all over the world compete in annual international competitions. These are the main ones.

The European Cup is played between the league champions of European countries. Since the competition began, in 1955, only 18 clubs have won it, with Spain's Real Madrid leading with six wins.

European Cup Winners' Cup is played between the winners of each country's national association cup. Held since 1960, English clubs have won it six times, and Spanish clubs five times.

The UEFA Cup involves clubs who have finished high in their country's national league and have not qualified for either of the other two European cups. Held since 1971, English clubs have won five times, West German clubs four times.

The European Super Cup is played for by the winners of the European Cup and European Cup Winners' Cup.

The Copa de Libertadores is played between the champions, runners-up and other highly placed teams from each of the South American national leagues.

The Concacaf Champions' Cup is played for by the champions of each Concacaf country. Held since 1963, Mexican clubs have dominated the competition.

The World Club Championship is a match played between the winners or runners-up of the European Cup and the winners of the Copa de Libertadores.

Index

First published in 1981 by Usborne Publishing Ltd, Usborne House, 83-85 Saffron Hill, London EC1N 8RT, England

This edition published 1993.

Text and artwork © 1993, 1986, 1981 Usborne Publishing Ltd.

The name Usborne and the device 🎈 are Trade Marks of Usborne Publishing Ltd.